Thanksgiving Jokes for Kids

By Riley Weber

RileyWeberArt.com

What key has legs and can't open doors?

A turkey!

What sound does a space turkey make?

Hubble, Hubble, Hubble!

Why did the turkey play drums in his band?

Because he already had drumsticks!

Who is not hungry at Thanksgiving?

The turkey, because he's already stuffed!

What type of music did the Pilgrims like?

Plymouth Rock!

What did the turkey say to the turkey hunter?

"Quack, quack, quack!"

If April showers bring May flowers, what do May flowers bring?

Pilgrims!

Why do turkeys always go, "Gobble, gobble"?

Because they never learned good table manners!

Why can't you take a turkey to church?

Because they use such fowl language!

What happened when the turkey got into a fight?

He got the stuffing knocked out of him!

Can a turkey jump higher than the Empire State Building?

Yes. A building can't jump at all!

Why did the turkey cross the road?

It was the chicken's day off!

When did the Pilgrims first say
"God bless America"?

When they first heard America sneeze!

Why did Johnny get such low grades after Thanksgiving?

Because everything is marked down
after the holidays!

What's the best dance to do on Thanksgiving?

The turkey trot!

What did the Turkey say before it was roasted?

Boy, I'm stuffed!

Why did the turkey sit on the tomahawk?

To try to hatchet!

How do you keep a turkey in suspense?

I'll let you know next week!

What's the best thing to put into pumpkin pie?

Your teeth!

What vegetables would you like with your Thanksgiving dinner?

Beets me!

What smells the best at a Thanksgiving dinner?

Your nose!

What always comes at the end of Thanksgiving?

The letter G!

THE END

More fun books for kids by Riley Weber…

Funny Jokes
(Silly short jokes that are colorfully illustrated for kids)

Funny Tongue Twisters for Kids
(New hilarious and challenging tongue twisters for children -all with cartoon pictures.)

Christmas Jokes
(Funny illustrated jokes about Santa, snowmen, Christmas trees, Yeti's, and much more)

Christmas Tongue Twisters for Kids
(Illustrated Tongue Twisters about Santa, snowmen, snowflakes, egg nog, presents, and much more.)

Knock Knock Jokes
(Knock knock jokes like you've never seen before. Illustrated. Every one of them. 50 plus pages of funny knock knock jokes for kids)

Valentines Riddles
(Fun illustrated collection of Valentines riddles to entertain and stimulate the imagination of children, bringing smiles to their faces)

Tongue Twisters
(50 new and challenging tongue twisters to give your tongue some exercises. These are like push-ups for the tongue. Every one features a silly cartoony illustration)

Halloween Jokes for Kids
(Hilarious haunted jokes for children about Dracula, candy, costumes, pumpkins, and more!)

Made in the USA
Las Vegas, NV
14 November 2022